You're Amazing, Anna Hibiscus!

Books by Atinuke:

Anna Hibiscus

Hooray for Anna Hibiscus!

Good Luck, Anna Hibiscus!

Have Fun, Anna Hibiscus!

Welcome Home, Anna Hibiscus!

Go Well, Anna Hibiscus!

Love from Anna Hibiscus!

You're Amazing, Anna Hibiscus!

For younger readers:

Double Trouble for Anna Hibiscus

You're Amazing, ANNA HIBISCUS!

by Atinuke

Illustrated by Lauren Tobia

Kane Miller
A DIVISION OF EDC PUBLISHING

First American Edition 2017
Kane Miller, A Division of EDC Publishing

First published in 2016 by Walker Books Ltd., London (England)

For information contact:
Kane Miller, A Division of EDC Publishing
P.O. Box 470663
Tulsa, OK 74147-0663
www.kanemiller.com
www.edcpub.com
usbornebooksandmore.com

Library of Congress Control Number: 2016961413

Printed and bound in the United States of America
1 2 3 4 5 6 7 8 9 10
ISBN: 978-1-61067-681-6

For my Amazing Aunts,
Susan, Alison, Judith, Catherine and Brigit,
who've taught me about love, courage,
friendship and loyalty.
Thank you!
A.

For Sophie Burdess,
a massive thank you.
L.T.

Double Trouble

Anna Hibiscus lives in Africa. Amazing Africa. She lives with her mother and her father, her grandmother and her grandfather, her aunties and her uncles, her cousins and her brothers and her best friend, Sunny Belafonte. They all live together in a big white house on the beautiful continent of Africa.

Anna Hibiscus's brothers are small. Anna Hibiscus's brothers are twins. This means trouble – double trouble!

Double and Trouble walk into trouble. Double and Trouble run into trouble. But most of all Double and Trouble climb into trouble. Double Trouble!

Double Trouble think trouble is funny. When they get into trouble they laugh. Then they point at each other.

"It was him! He did it!" They both laugh.

But sometimes somebody else gets the blame!

One day Double Trouble climbed to the top of the high cupboard where Uncle Tunde kept his camera. Double Trouble loved cameras!

They loved to press all the buttons and see the lights on the screen flash! They loved to take photographs too!

"Stop!" said Anna Hibiscus when she came into the room.

Anna Hibiscus carefully put the camera back. She hoped Double Trouble hadn't deleted any of Uncle Tunde's important photographs.

That weekend Uncle Tunde's friends came to visit. Uncle Tunde got his camera down and pressed SLIDESHOW. He wanted his friends to see all the photographs of his engineering project.

But all Uncle Tunde's friends saw were Double Trouble's funny faces and Double Trouble's fat bom-boms! They laughed and laughed.

But Uncle Tunde was cross. He was cross with Double Trouble.

"It was him! He did it!" Double pointed at Trouble.

"It was him! He did it!" Trouble pointed at Double.

"It was both of you!" said Anna Hibiscus. "I saw you!"

Now Uncle Tunde was cross with Anna Hibiscus. "You should have stopped them!" he said.

"I tried!" said Anna Hibiscus.

But Uncle Tunde was still cross.

The next day Double Trouble climbed onto the table. They found Joy's schoolbag. Inside they found face paints! Double

Trouble loved face paints. And Joy had the very best kind!

When Anna Hibiscus saw Double
Trouble's faces she laughed. Then she asked,
"Where did you get those fine-fine face
paints?"

Anna Hibiscus wanted face paints too, but
Double Trouble wouldn't answer.

"Double Trouble have face paints!" Anna
Hibiscus shouted.

All the aunties came running.

"That looks like lipstick!" said Auntie Joly.

"And eye shadow!" said Auntie Grace.

"Where did you get them?" asked Anna's
mother.

Double Trouble pointed to Joy's bag.
Then they pointed at each other.

"It was him! He did it!"
Double laughed.

"It was him! He did it!"
Trouble laughed louder.

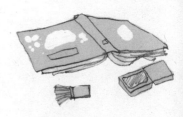

But the aunties were not looking at Double
Trouble. They were looking at Joy. Girl
cousins were not allowed to have makeup.

Now it was Joy who was in trouble!
Auntie Joly took away the lipstick and the
eye shadow. Joy cried. "Why did you have
to call everybody!" she shouted at Anna
Hibiscus. "Now I have lost my makeup!"

Poor Anna Hibiscus.

She was in trouble again!

Every-every day Double Trouble caused
trouble for Anna Hibiscus!

They pulled down the shower curtain
when Anna's mother was in the shower.

"Why didn't you stop them, Anna?"
shouted Anna's
mother.

They climbed into
the fridge and spilled the stew.

"I told you to keep them out of the
kitchen, Anna!" shouted Uncle Bizi Sunday.

They climbed onto the cousins' beds and
pulled their posters off the wall.

"It's your fault, Anna!" cried Chocolate
and Angel. "They're your brothers!"

Now Anna Hibiscus was so cross that she shouted at Double Trouble. "You're always getting me into trouble! It's not fair! I wish you weren't my brothers!"

Double and Trouble were sad. They didn't care if other people were cross with them, but they didn't want Anna Hibiscus to be cross. Anna was their sister. And they loved her.

Anna Hibiscus loved Double Trouble too. When she saw their sad faces she was sorry for what she said!

Double Trouble looked at Anna Hibiscus. Anna Hibiscus looked at Double Trouble. They were all sad and they did not know what to do to make it better.

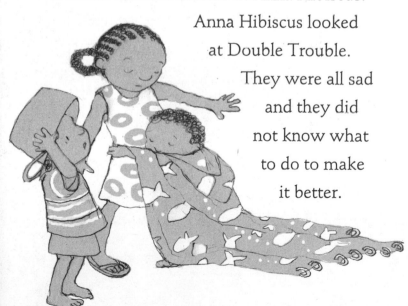

The next day the big
white house was quiet and
empty. Cousins were at
school. Uncles were
at work. Aunties
were shopping.
Grandmother and
Grandfather had gone
to see the doctor.
Uncle Bizi Sunday
went to market. He
slammed the door
behind him and it
locked.

Anna Hibiscus and
the bigger cousins came
home from school.
Nobody was home. And
the big white house was shut and locked.
Had anybody got the key? The one old key
for the old-old lock to the big white house?

The cousins didn't have the key. They never had the key. Children were not allowed to touch the one old key for the old-old lock.

The aunties came home from shopping with the little cousins. The big cousins were waiting in the garden. The big white house was shut and locked! Did the aunties have the key? The one old key for the old-old lock?

No, the aunties didn't have the key!

The uncles came home from work. The cousins and aunties were waiting in the garden. The big white house was shut and locked!

Did the uncles have the key? The one old key for the old-old lock? No, the uncles didn't have the key!

Grandmother and Grandfather came home from the doctor. The cousins and aunties and uncles were waiting in the garden. The big white house was shut and locked!

Did Grandmother and Grandfather have the key? The one old key for the old-old lock to the big white house? No, Grandmother and Grandfather didn't have the key!

The cousins looked at the aunties. "Did you not take the key when you went shopping?" asked the cousins.

"We never take the key!" said the aunties.

"There is always somebody home when we get back from shopping!"

The aunties looked at the uncles. "Why did you not take the key when you went to work?" they asked.

"We never take the key!" said the uncles. "There is always somebody here when we get home from work!"

The uncles looked at Grandmother and Grandfather. "Did you not take the key when you went to the doctor?" they asked.

"We never take the key!" said Grandmother and Grandfather. "There is always somebody here when we get home!"

Grandmother and Grandfather looked at Uncle Bizi Sunday. "Why did you not take the key?" they asked. "You were the last one to leave."

"I did not know that you people had all gone out!" said Uncle Bizi Sunday. "There is always somebody here in the big white house! Why should I take the key?"

The cousins and aunties and uncles and Grandmother and Grandfather looked at one another. The big white house was shut and locked. The only key was inside, hanging on a hook in the kitchen.

The uncles walked around the house, looking for an open window. But all the windows were closed. All except one, but that window was high. Too high up to reach. The uncles groaned.

Anna Hibiscus started to cry. She was hot and tired and thirsty and she did not like being locked out of the big white house.

Double Trouble looked at each other. How could they stop Anna Hibiscus from crying? If they could make her smile, she would want them to be her brothers again.

Double Trouble saw a window. A tiny open window hidden by the beautiful purple bougainvillea flowers growing on the wall.

"Shh!" the uncles said to Anna Hibiscus. "Stop crying! We are phoning for help."

Anna Hibiscus tried to stop crying. She looked at the wall of the big white house. It was covered with purple bougainvillea flowers. Anna Hibiscus looked at the flowers. They were moving and shaking!

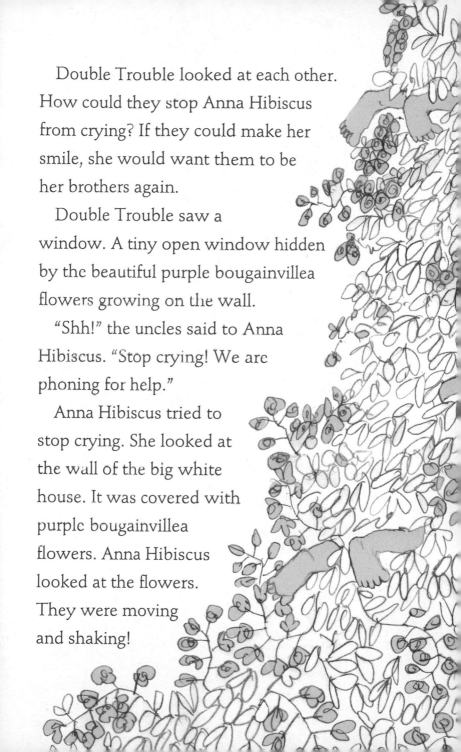

Anna Hibiscus stared at the shaking purple
flowers. The cousins saw Anna Hibiscus
staring. They looked at the flowers too.

The aunties saw the cousins staring. The
aunties looked up at the purple flowers too.

The uncles saw the aunties pointing.
The uncles looked up at the shaking purple
bougainvillea.

Grandmother and Grandfather saw the
uncles drop their phones. They looked
up at the purple flowers. They saw them
shaking too!

Everybody in Anna Hibiscus's family was
staring at the shaking purple bougainvillea.
Suddenly a small hand appeared from
the flowers. Anna Hibiscus's
mother gasped.

The hand
grasped the high
window that
the uncles

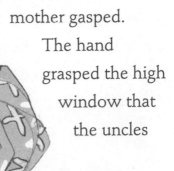

had not noticed, an open window into the hallway of the big white house.

Double climbed out of the flowers and in through the open window high in the wall.

Anna Hibiscus's whole family had wide-open mouths.

Then Trouble climbed out of the bougainvillea and in through the open window high in the wall.

"Be careful!" Mama shouted.

There was a crash.

Grandmother closed her eyes. "That was my vase!" she cried. "It was on the windowsill."

There was another crash.

"That was my trophy!" Grandfather groaned. "It was next to the vase!"

There was silence, then lots of crashing. Everybody jumped.

"What are they doing?" shouted Uncle Eldest.

"They are going to break everything!" cried Auntie Joly.

"Now they are locked in the house all alone!" wailed Anna's mother.

The aunties clutched their heads. The uncles groaned. Grandmother had her hand over her mouth.

"Those boys are trouble!" said Uncle Eldest.

"Double Trouble!" Anna's father groaned.

Suddenly a hand appeared in the window and Double climbed out, into the flowers.

Trouble climbed out into the flowers too. Now the bougainvillea was shaking again, until out of the bottom tumbled Double and Trouble.

The whole family opened their mouths
to shout – everybody except Anna Hibiscus.
Anna Hibiscus closed her
eyes. She wondered
how she was going
to be blamed for this
new trouble.

Suddenly Anna
Hibiscus felt something
in her hand, and she
opened her eyes. It was
the one old key to the old-old lock of the
big white house. And there were Double
Trouble looking at her and smiling.

"For you, Anna," Double
Trouble said. "Can we be
your brothers again?"

"Look!" Anna Hibiscus
waved the key.

The family gasped and
shouted and cheered.

25

Anna Hibiscus put her arms around her brothers. "I'm sorry for what I said. I'm glad you are my brothers. No matter what!"

"No matter what trouble?" asked Trouble.

"No matter double trouble?" asked Double.

"No matter what!" said Anna Hibiscus.

 Trouble snatched the key from Anna's hand. Double threw it up into the air.

"Anna Hibiscus, why did you let them snatch the key?" Auntie Joly shouted.

The aunties and uncles and cousins shouted and jumped up to catch the key.

The key spun higher and higher through the air.

The uncles fell over the aunties. The aunties fell over the cousins. The cousins fell over one another and the one old key fell into Grandfather's lap. The whole entire family lay tangled on the ground!

Double and Trouble laughed and laughed and laughed, then they stopped. They looked at Anna Hibiscus. Was she going to be cross with them again?

No! Anna Hibiscus was laughing too!

Good-bye, Grandfather

Anna Hibiscus was worried. Her mother and father were worried. The aunties and uncles were worried. The cousins were worried. Even Sunny Belafonte was worried.

Everybody was worried because Grandfather was tired.

Grandfather was so tired that he did not get up from his mat. He did not go onto the balcony with the uncles. He did not go onto the veranda with Grandmother. Grandfather used to love to do those things, but now he was too tired.

Grandfather was so tired he did not eat with the family. He said it was too noisy. He did not read his newspapers anymore. He said they were too heavy. He did not want to listen to anybody else reading them. He said it was too tiring.

All Grandfather wanted to do was sit on his mat. All he wanted to do was lean on Grandmother.

Grandmother smiled. She stroked Grandfather's face. She patted Grandfather's hand.

"Grandfather is tired because he is old," Grandmother told everybody. "And there is nothing wrong with being old."

Grandfather tried to smile, but
Grandfather was too tired even to smile.

Now Grandfather was too tired even
to lean on Grandmother. All Grandfather
wanted to do now was lie on his
mat and sleep.

The aunties and uncles and cousins took it
in turns to sit with Grandfather. They took
it in turns to hold his hand. They stroked his
face. They whispered to him.

"Sleep well, Baba," the uncles whispered.
"Wake up strong."

"We are praying for you, Baba," the aunties
whispered. "Soon you will be strong."

"Wake up, wake up," the cousins
whispered.

But Anna Hibiscus did not sit with Grandfather. Anna Hibiscus did not hold Grandfather's hand.

Anna Hibiscus played in the garden with Sunny Belafonte. They ran and climbed trees. Anna Hibiscus was pretending that nothing had changed in the big white house. She was pretending that she was not worried.

Anna's mother tapped on the window. "Come in, Anna!" she shouted. "Come in and sit with Grandfather."

Anna Hibiscus shook her head. She was far too worried to do that! And she wanted to pretend that there was nothing to worry about.

Anna Hibiscus's father called from the door. "Come in, Anna!" he shouted. "Come in and hold Grandfather's hand."

Anna Hibiscus shook her head. She was far too worried to do that!

Uncle Tunde went out into the garden. "Come in, Anna Hibiscus!" he called. "Come in and talk to Grandfather."

Anna Hibiscus shook her head. She was far too worried to do that! Outside in the garden Anna could forget that inside the house everybody was whispering. She could forget that inside everybody was worrying. She could forget that something bad could happen!

Inside the big white house Grandfather sometimes woke up. He whispered too.

"I love you," he whispered to Grandmother. "Thank you for everything, *ore mi* dear."

"Do not worry," he whispered to the uncles. "You have always done the right thing.

"Do not cry," he whispered to the aunties. "You have always made me proud of you.

"I am an old man now," he whispered to the cousins. "I need to sleep." And sometimes he whispered, "Where is Anna Hibiscus?"

"She is in the garden." Grandmother smiled.

"Climbing trees!" Auntie Joly sniffed.

"Running around!" Uncle Eldest frowned.

"Laughing!" whispered the cousins in shocked voices.

And it was then that Grandfather smiled. He smiled his big wide smile, a smile as big and as beautiful as Africa. "Amazing Anna Hibiscus," he said.

Then one day Grandfather did not wake up anymore. He was not sleeping now.

Grandmother looked at Grandfather. The aunties and uncles and cousins looked at Grandfather.

Now the big white house was not full of whispers anymore. Now it was full of crying and wailing and sobbing.

Anna Hibiscus heard the crying and
wailing and sobbing. All of a sudden Anna
Hibiscus was afraid. She was afraid that
the really bad thing had happened. Anna
Hibiscus ran into the big white house. She
wanted to sit with Grandfather. She wanted
to hold Grandfather's hand. She wanted to
whisper to Grandfather.

Grandmother held out her arms to
Anna Hibiscus. Anna Hibiscus ran into
Grandmother's arms. She looked at
Grandfather lying on his mat. Anna Hibiscus
could see that Grandfather
was not sleeping now.
Anna Hibiscus
started to cry. "Wake
him up!" Anna
Hibiscus
sobbed. "Make
Grandfather
wake up!"

"Anna Hibiscus," Grandmother said, "Grandfather's body is too old and weak to wake up." Tears rolled down Grandmother's cheeks.

Anna Hibiscus thought she knew what that meant. It meant the really bad thing had happened. The thing that was too bad to think about. The thing she pretended would never happen.

But maybe Anna Hibiscus was wrong. Could she still be wrong? "Will Grandfather wake up one day?" Anna Hibiscus asked.

Grandmother shook her head. "Grandfather will never wake up."

"Does that mean Grandfather—?" Anna sobbed loudly.

"Yes, Anna Hibiscus." Grandmother nodded. "Grandfather has died."

Anna Hibiscus's heart cracked. "But I did not sit with him." Anna sobbed louder. "I did not hold his hand. I did not say good-bye!"

"You said good-bye in your own way,"
Grandmother said as she held Anna Hibiscus
very tightly, "by playing in the garden. That
made Grandfather very happy."

Anna Hibiscus did not believe
Grandmother. She did not believe
Grandmother for one second.

At Grandfather's funeral Anna Hibiscus
did not stop crying. The aunties and uncles
and cousins did not stop crying. Even
Grandmother cried and wailed and sobbed.

After the funeral many people came to the big white house. They were all crying and wailing and sobbing, and eating too. Anna Hibiscus wished that they would all go away.

Anna Hibiscus did not know what to do with herself. Everywhere she went was some place Grandfather should have been!

He should have been sitting on his mat in the sitting room with Grandmother.

He should have been on the balcony, discussing the news with the uncles.

He should have been on the veranda, reading his newspapers and supervising the compound.

He should have been where Anna Hibiscus could talk to him! Anna sobbed and sobbed. She could hear the big girl cousins whispering.

"Grandfather was always asking for Anna," said Joy.

"And she would never come," said Clarity.

"She did not love him enough," said Common Sense.

Anna Hibiscus's heart cracked wide-open. It hurt so much that Anna Hibiscus screamed.

Anna Hibiscus's father ran to Anna and held her in his arms.

"What have those silly girls been saying?" he asked Anna Hibiscus.

Anna Hibiscus said nothing. The pain in her heart was too terrible for her to speak.

Is that what Grandfather thought in the end? That Anna Hibiscus did not love him?

"Do you know what made Grandfather happy?" her father asked. "Do you know what made him happy in the end?"

Still Anna Hibiscus said nothing.

"It was not people holding his hand or whispering to him about all the things that they wanted which he could no longer do for them."

Still Anna Hibiscus said nothing.

"It was you, Anna Hibiscus," her father said. "It was you who made him happy in the end. It was the thought of you running and playing and laughing in this garden that he made. That is what made Grandfather happy at the end of his life."

Anna Hibiscus looked into her father's eyes. She searched for the truth. "Really?" Anna whispered.

"I promise you," her father said. "I promise this is true."

Anna's father put her gently on the ground.

"You could not have loved Grandfather more," he said. "You know that and he knew that. Don't let anybody tell you any different."

Anna Hibiscus felt better. A bit better. She did not go back to the house with her father. She did not want to be where Grandfather was not.

Anna Hibiscus leaned her face against the white wall of the garden. "Grandfather, where are you?" Anna cried.

"Grandfather is still here," Grandmother said gently.

Anna Hibiscus turned around. Grandmother was standing there.

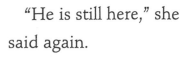

"He is still here," she said again.

"He's not here!" Anna shouted.

"Anna Hibiscus," Grandmother said gently. "Everything that made Grandfather Grandfather is still here – his jokes the uncles tell, his stories that the aunties know, the things he taught us that we all remember. It is all still here. It is only his body that is gone."

"He is not here!" Anna shouted louder.

"His body grew old, Anna," Grandmother continued. "But you can still hear him. If you listen..."

"I can't see him!" Anna Hibiscus shouted even louder. "And I can't hear him!"

"You can't see him," Grandmother agreed. "But you can hear him, in here." Grandmother leaned over and tapped Anna's heart.

Anna opened her mouth to shout again.

"Maybe if you stop shouting you will hear him," said Grandmother.

Anna Hibiscus closed her mouth.

"Close your eyes," said Grandmother. "Close your eyes and speak to Grandfather in your heart."

Anna Hibiscus frowned. But she closed her eyes. "Grandfather?" Anna whispered in her heart.

"It is not good to shout at your Grandmother," Grandfather said in Anna's heart.

Anna Hibiscus opened her eyes! She heard Grandfather's voice! She heard Grandfather speaking in her heart!

Grandmother smiled at Anna Hibiscus. Anna closed her eyes again. "Why did you leave me, Grandfather?" her heart cried out. "I need you."

"I taught you all that I could, Anna Hibiscus," Grandfather's voice said. "You know everything you need to know. You do not need me anymore."

"I do," cried Anna's heart. "I do need you. I miss you."

"I am here," said Grandfather.

And suddenly Anna Hibiscus felt Grandfather's love all around her. Her eyes opened again.

"He's here!" she whispered. "I can feel him!"

Grandmother smiled again. She stroked the top of Anna's head, then she walked back to the house. "Amazing Anna," she said.

Anna Hibiscus stayed by the wall for a long time, listening to Grandfather. "I wish

I had said good-bye, Grandfather," Anna said.

"You did not need to say good-bye, Anna Hibiscus," Grandfather answered. "I am still here. We can talk like this for as long as you like."

"Forever?" asked Anna Hibiscus.

"For as long as you need me," said Grandfather.

"Forever," said Anna Hibiscus.

What's Wrong, Sunny?

Anna Hibiscus lives with her mother and her father and her grandmother. She lives with her aunties and her uncles. She lives with her cousins and her brothers and her best friend, Sunny Belafonte.

Sunny Belafonte and Anna Hibiscus's
grandfathers were best friends too. Sunny
Belafonte used to live with his grandfather.
After Sunny's grandfather died, Sunny
Belafonte came to live with Anna Hibiscus.

Now that Anna Hibiscus's grandfather has
died too, he did not live with Anna Hibiscus
in the big white house. Now Grandfather
lived in Anna Hibiscus's heart.

When Anna Hibiscus
wanted to talk to Grandfather
she went somewhere quiet,
somewhere so quiet
that she could hear
Grandfather's voice
whispering in her
heart.

It was not often
quiet in the big white
house. Cousins were often quarreling,
aunties were often shouting and uncles

were often turning up the radio. Anna Hibiscus had to go into the garden to hear Grandfather's voice.

At school it was even louder than at the big white house. School was so busy and noisy and loud that Anna Hibiscus couldn't hear Grandfather's voice at-all, at-all.

At school Anna Hibiscus felt as though Grandfather was utterly gone. All Anna Hibiscus could feel was how sad and angry she was.

At playtime Anna Hibiscus stood by the fence. When Anna Hibiscus's friends came to stand with her, Anna Hibiscus shouted at them to go away.

"I don't like you anymore!" Anna Hibiscus shouted.

Anna Hibiscus's friends looked sad and confused. Anna Hibiscus was glad. She wanted other people to feel sad. She wanted other people to feel how she was feeling.

Anna Hibiscus looked around the playground. Some children were pushing and shouting at somebody. Those children were always being mean. Anna had never played with them before, but now Anna Hibiscus wanted to be mean too.

Anna Hibiscus ran over to the pushing, shouting children.

"Bush boy! Bush boy!" they were saying.

Anna Hibiscus said it too. "Bush boy! Bush boy!"

Anna Hibiscus shouted louder and louder and louder. Anna Hibiscus pushed harder

and harder and harder. It made Anna
Hibiscus feel better to do something with
the sadness in her heart.

Suddenly Anna Hibiscus pushed her way
right to the front. Her hands landed on the
back of the boy the children were pushing.
When Anna Hibiscus pushed him, the
boy fell to the ground. Then Anna
Hibiscus saw – the boy was Sunny
Belafonte. Sunny Belafonte,
her best friend!

Anna Hibiscus felt sick. She
felt so sick that the teacher sent
her home.

At home Grandmother looked
at Anna Hibiscus. She told
everybody to leave Anna Hibiscus alone.
Anna Hibiscus sat by the compound wall
with her back to the big white house. It
was quiet. But it was not quiet inside Anna
Hibiscus.

Inside Anna Hibiscus her heart was wailing. It was crying too loudly for Anna to hear Grandfather's voice. Anna Hibiscus was glad. She did not want to hear what Grandfather would say about what she had done.

Anna Hibiscus felt ashamed. Anna Hibiscus felt guilty. They were the worst feelings that Anna Hibiscus had ever felt, worse than sadness and worse than sorrow and even worse than anger.

Anna Hibiscus heard Uncle Tunde's car. He was bringing the cousins and Sunny home from school. Anna Hibiscus made herself as small as she could. She waited for Sunny Belafonte to tell everybody what she did at school.

Nothing happened. Only Grandmother

came to see Anna Hibiscus. She put her hand on Anna's head. "What does Grandfather say today?" Grandmother asked.

Anna Hibiscus cried out. She ran away from Grandmother. She hid in her room and refused to leave.

The next morning Anna Hibiscus refused to go to school. She said she was sick.

"Come on, Anna," said her mother. "You look fine to me."

But there was no time to say more because everybody was rushing around looking for Sunny Belafonte. He was not in the car. He was not in his bedroom. He was not anywhere.

"Let me take the others to school," said Uncle Tunde. "Then I will come back to look for the boy. Come on, Anna."

Anna Hibiscus shook her head. Grandmother looked closely at Anna Hibiscus. "She will stay at home today," she said.

Uncle Tunde took the others to school. Everybody else kept looking for Sunny Belafonte, but they couldn't find him.

Grandmother was seriously worried. "Who saw the boy last?" she asked.

"He did not want to eat, remember?" said Uncle Bizi Sunday.

"He went straight upstairs after school," said Auntie Grace.

Grandmother looked at Anna Hibiscus. "You too did not want to eat yesterday, Anna," she said. "And you too went upstairs early. What is going on?"

Anna Hibiscus thought she was going to be sick. She shook her head again.

"I blame myself." Grandmother's voice cracked. "I should have checked on the boy."

"You were busy checking on Anna," said Auntie Grace. "I should have checked on the boy."

"And me," said Auntie Joly.

"And me," said Uncle Bizi Sunday.

When Uncle Tunde returned he had news. "Common Sense checked on Sunny last night," he said. "He was in his room and he only spoke when she was leaving."

"What did Sunny say?" asked Grandmother.

"He said, 'When will I be sent back?'" said Uncle Tunde.

Everybody was silent.

"What made him think that we would send him back?" Grandmother's voice shook.

Anna Hibiscus burst into tears. Everybody stared at her.

"Anna Hibiscus!" said Grandmother fiercely. "What is going on?"

Anna Hibiscus had never seen Grandmother look or sound so fierce.

"This is serious, Anna!" her mother said.

So Anna Hibiscus told everybody what happened at school. Anna Hibiscus was so ashamed and so guilty that she wanted to disappear into the ground.

Everybody was silent when Anna Hibiscus stopped talking.

"The boy will try to return to his village," Grandmother said at last. "Tunde and Sunday, you must go and look for him." Then Grandmother said to Anna Hibiscus, "You will go too."

"But he hates me!" Anna cried. "He will run away again if he sees me."

"That is what you have to fix," said her father sternly.

"You must find a way to fix it or Sunny

will never return," said her mother sadly.

"Anna Hibiscus, listen to me," said Grandmother. "There is one decision all human beings have to make. It does not matter whether we are rich or poor or whether we are happy or sad. We all have to make the 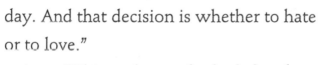 same decision every day. And that decision is whether to hate or to love."

Anna Hibiscus knew she had already made the wrong decision. And she did not know how to make it right. She did not want to get in the car. But she knew it would be worse to stay behind.

Anna Hibiscus set off with Uncle Tunde
and Uncle Bizi Sunday. The uncles discussed
which way to go and where to look. Anna
Hibiscus did not speak and nobody spoke
to her.

They did not find Sunny at the bus
station. They did not find him at the taxi
ranks. Uncle Tunde started to drive to
the village. It was a long way.
Nobody was speaking.

It was so quiet that suddenly Anna Hibiscus heard Grandfather speak in her heart. It was so sudden that she did not have time to silence him before she heard what he said.

"Now you know why people behave in mean and ugly ways, Anna Hibiscus," Grandfather said.

Anna Hibiscus was surprised.

"What do you mean, Grandfather?" she asked.

"You behaved in a mean and ugly way, Anna Hibiscus," Grandfather said. "So now you can understand why sometimes other people do the same."

Anna Hibiscus thought for a long time. Then she whispered back. "I was angry that you are dead, Grandfather, and that I was at school and that I could not even hear your voice. I was feeling bad. I wanted everybody to feel bad too."

"Exactly," said Grandfather.

"Is that why other people are mean?" Anna Hibiscus asked. "Because they are feeling bad and they want other people to feel bad too?"

"Yes," said Grandfather. "I believe that is so."

"But I did not want to be mean to Sunny," Anna cried. "I did not want him to feel bad!"

Grandfather was silent.

"Now everybody hates me," continued Anna. "Everybody thinks I am a mean and ugly and bad person."

"There is no such thing as a bad person, Anna Hibiscus," said Grandfather. "There are only good people who behave in mean and ugly ways because their hearts are feeling bad."

Then Uncle Bizi Sunday shouted, "There he is!"

Sunny Belafonte
was walking
beside the road.
He looked small
and tired and very,
very sad.

Uncle Tunde
stopped the car.
Sunny Belafonte
looked around. When he saw them he
started to run into the bush.

Anna Hibiscus jumped out of the car.
She ran after Sunny Belafonte.
Sunny Belafonte ran faster.

"Please, Sunny!" Anna
shouted. "Please stop!
I want to say sorry.
Please take my sorry,
Sunny."

Sunny Belafonte
kept running.

"I did not know it was you, Sunny!" Anna shouted. "I did not know that it was you I was pushing."

Sunny Belafonte stopped running. His nose was dripping. Tears were running from his eyes.

"I hate you!" he shouted. "I hate you, Anna Hibiscus."

"I hate me too!" Anna Hibiscus shouted back. Sunny Belafonte looked surprised.

"I was feeling bad because Grandfather

is dead," added Anna. "I wanted somebody else to feel bad too. But not you, Sunny! I did not know it was you."

Anna Hibiscus started to cry.

"We all love you, Sunny," said Uncle Tunde, panting.

"Even Auntie Joly." Uncle Bizi Sunday was panting too.

Sunny Belafonte looked surprised again. Auntie Joly was always so cross.

"We want you to come home, Sunny," said Uncle Tunde. "We all do. Even Auntie Joly."

"The quicker you come the better," said Uncle Bizi Sunday. "The longer you take, the more Auntie Joly will worry. And the more she worries, the more cross she will become."

Sunny Belafonte nearly smiled. He got into the car with Anna Hibiscus and Uncle Tunde and Uncle Bizi Sunday.

On the way home Anna asked again, "Will you take my sorry, Sunny?"

Sunny Belafonte nodded. "When my mother and grandfather died I felt bad and I was bad too," he said. "Badder than you."

Anna Hibiscus squeezed Sunny's hand. She had forgotten that Sunny knew all about people dying.

Grandmother and the aunties and uncles and cousins were so happy to see Sunny Belafonte again. He had never had so many kisses in his life. Only Auntie Joly was cross.

"Did you want to give me a heart attack?" she shouted. "Did you want to kill me?"

Sunny Belafonte smiled. He put his arms around Auntie Joly.

"I love you," he said.

Auntie Joly opened and closed her mouth several times. She looked so surprised that everybody laughed.

Then Auntie Joly hugged Sunny back.

"I love you too," she whispered in his ear.

Then everybody else looked surprised too. Grandmother smiled, then she spoke again.

"I will write to the school," she said, "and tell them that I am reconsidering sending our children to a school that allows such bullying as Sunny has suffered."

Everybody nodded.

"Will you be a witness, Anna Hibiscus?"
Grandmother asked.

Anna Hibiscus swallowed. Being a witness
meant admitting that she too had been a
bully. Being a witness meant that the bullies
might turn on her next.

"Being a witness," said Grandfather's voice
in her heart, "is a chance to right the wrong
that you did."

Anna Hibiscus held her
head up high.

"I will," she said.

Everybody smiled.

"Well done!" said
Grandfather in Anna's
heart.

Sunny Belafonte
squeezed Anna's
hand. "You're
amazing, Anna
Hibiscus," he said.

And for the first time since Grandfather had died, Anna Hibiscus smiled.

No More Trouble

Anna Hibiscus lives in Africa, amazing Africa, with almost her whole entire family, her best friend, Sunny Belafonte, and her two brothers, Double and Trouble.

Double and Trouble used to like running. They used to like climbing. They used to like trouble.

Double and Trouble used to walk into trouble. They used to run into trouble. They used to climb into trouble.

Now Double and Trouble lie on the grass and watch ants. They lie under the kitchen table and count grains of rice. They lie in their bed and do not climb out.

Double and Trouble don't get into any trouble at-all, at-all. And Double and Trouble don't laugh at-all, at-all.

Anna Hibiscus's mother and father and aunties and uncles were worried about Double Trouble.

"Maybe they need a tonic," said Anna's mother.

"Maybe they need an outing to the zoo," said Anna's father.

"Maybe they need a job," said Auntie Joly.

Trouble swallowed the tonic. Double spat it out. But it did not make them climb into trouble and laugh again. Double Trouble stayed lying in their bed. The doctor came to check them, and he said nothing was wrong!

So Anna's father took them to the zoo. Trouble stared at the monkeys in the zoo. Double closed his eyes. But the monkeys did not make them climb into trouble and laugh again.

So Auntie Joly
gave Double Trouble
a job. Trouble fed
the chickens every
morning. Double
did not bother. But
the job did not make
them climb into trouble
and laugh again.

"What are we
going to do?" asked
Anna's mother.

Anna's father
shook his head.
All the aunties shook their heads.
Even Grandmother shook her head.

Nobody knew what to do about Double
Trouble. Everybody wanted them to run and
climb and laugh again,
even if it meant that
they got into trouble!

Anna Hibiscus
climbed onto
Grandmother's lap.
"I talk to Grandfather
every day," Anna said,
"and I still feel sad."

Grandmother
looked at Anna Hibiscus. She stroked her
hair. "One day the sadness will go, Anna
Hibiscus," she said.

"No." Anna Hibiscus shook her head.
"I am going to be sad forever!"

Grandmother smiled. "It will take time,"
she said. Then Grandmother sighed.

"Are you sad too, Grandmother?" Anna
asked.

"Yes," said Grandmother. "And I am
worried too."

"Why, Grandmother?" Anna asked.

"I am worried about them." Grandmother
pointed to Double Trouble.

Anna Hibiscus looked at Double Trouble. They were not running. They were not climbing. They were not causing trouble. They were lying on the grass, watching ants.

"What's wrong with Double Trouble?" Anna asked.

"Nobody knows." Grandmother sighed again. "They are too small to tell us."

Anna Hibiscus looked at Double Trouble. They looked so small and so sad. Anna Hibiscus was worried now too. Double Trouble were too small to be sad!

Anna Hibiscus climbed off Grandmother's lap. She marched towards Double Trouble. Anna Hibiscus was going to do something about this! Grandmother smiled.

"Hello, Trouble," said Anna. "Hello, Double."

Double Trouble looked at Anna Hibiscus.

"Would you like me to sing to you?" asked Anna Hibiscus.

Trouble shook his head. Double shrugged. Maybe they didn't remember that her songs always cheered them up. Anna Hibiscus sang a song anyway.

Though Anna Hibiscus sang all her songs, Double and Trouble did not cheer up. Now Anna Hibiscus was worried. Something must be very wrong with Double Trouble.

"Do your tummies hurt?" she asked.

Double Trouble shook their heads.

"Do your throats hurt?" Anna asked.

Double Trouble shook their heads again.

"Does anything hurt?" Anna asked.

Double Trouble shrugged.

"What?" Anna Hibiscus asked. "What hurts?"

Double Trouble shrugged again. Then they got up and went into the kitchen to lie under the table.

Anna Hibiscus followed Double Trouble. She found Uncle Bizi Sunday in the kitchen, slowly stirring a stew.

"Something is wrong with Double Trouble," Anna said.

Uncle Bizi Sunday looked at Double Trouble and sighed. "Maybe they are tired," he said. "I am tired."

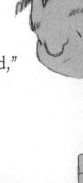

Anna Hibiscus frowned. Anna Hibiscus left Double Trouble counting rice. She left Uncle Bizi Sunday stirring stew. She went into the sewing room. The aunties were there, hemming cloth.

"Something is wrong with Double Trouble," Anna Hibiscus said.

The aunties sighed. "There is always something wrong with somebody," they said.

Anna Hibiscus frowned.

Anna Hibiscus left the aunties sighing. She went upstairs to the big cousins' room. The big cousins were staring at their homework books.

"Something is wrong with Double Trouble," Anna said.

One of the big cousins put his head on his book.

"Another unsolvable problem," he said.

Anna Hibiscus frowned again.

Anna Hibiscus left the cousins staring at their books. She went back downstairs and sat down halfway. She knew the uncles were on the balcony, but she couldn't hear their voices. That was strange. The uncles were always discussing and debating.

"I wish I had something to keep myself occupied." Anna Hibiscus heard her father sigh.

This was serious. There was not just something wrong with Double Trouble, there was something wrong with everybody in the big white house!

Anna Hibiscus got up. She went outside and climbed the mango tree. It was the best place to think.

From the mango tree Anna Hibiscus
could see Grandmother on the veranda.
Grandmother was dozing with her head
bobbing backwards and forwards. Anna
Hibiscus did not want to wake her up. She
did not want to worry her even more.

"Oh, Grandfather!" Anna Hibiscus sighed.
"Why aren't you here to tell me what to do!"

The wind rustled the leaves of the mango
tree and Grandfather's voice whispered in
Anna's heart. And Anna Hibiscus knew
what to do. She jumped down from the tree.

Anna Hibiscus ran
and put a pillow under
Grandmother's head.
Grandmother sighed
happily. Anna Hibiscus
smiled.

Anna Hibiscus ran up to the
balcony. The uncles were there, sighing.

"The cousins need help with their
homework," Anna said.

"Of course!" The uncles jumped up from
their chairs.

Anna Hibiscus smiled.

She ran back downstairs. She went into

the kitchen and took
the spoon from
Uncle Bizi Sunday.

"I can stir that,"
she said to Uncle Bizi
Sunday. "The aunties
are lonely."

Anna Hibiscus stirred the stew. Uncle Bizi Sunday went to put his feet up in the sewing room. Anna heard the aunties laugh at one of his funny-funny jokes. Anna Hibiscus smiled.

Then Anna Hibiscus looked at Double Trouble. Suddenly Anna Hibiscus stopped smiling. Anna Hibiscus still did not know what to do about Double Trouble!

Double Trouble looked at Anna Hibiscus. Then Trouble asked, "Grandfather?"

Anna Hibiscus dropped the spoon. Her cracked heart almost broke in two. Anna Hibiscus sat down on the floor.

"Grandfather?" Double asked.

Anna Hibiscus did not know what to say. She did not want to say that Grandfather was dead. Double Trouble knew that already. She did not want to explain that that meant he was never coming back. That was too hard to say and too sad to hear. She could not explain about listening to Grandfather in their hearts. Double Trouble were too small to understand.

Double Trouble looked at Anna Hibiscus and waited.

Suddenly something came into Anna Hibiscus's head. It was something that somebody told her once when she was on her way to Canada and missing her family.

"Once upon a time, Grandfather was a small boy," Anna Hibiscus began.

Double Trouble's eyes opened wide.

"He lived in the village. And he had to collect firewood so that his mother could cook his food. There was no gas. There was no electricity."

Double Trouble listened.

"Grandfather loved to eat his mother's food. He was a hungry boy."

Double Trouble nodded. They were always hungry too!

"Grandfather also loved to play. He loved to play more than he loved to work."

Double Trouble looked at each other and nodded again.

"He never remembered to collect firewood until he was hungry."

Double Trouble smiled.

"One day Grandfather was very hungry. He ran to collect firewood. It took him a long time. He was so hungry and wished he had gone sooner!"

Double Trouble listened. They nodded. They smiled.

"Grandfather was walking back to the village with the firewood on his head. Suddenly he felt something crawling in his hair."

Double Trouble's eyes opened wide!

"Grandfather wanted to drop the firewood, but he knew if he did, it would take longer before his mother could cook food. Grandfather was so hungry that he just kept walking."

Double and Trouble scratched their heads.

"Grandfather could feel things crawling in his hair and down his back. Grandfather shouted 'Aieee!' and he ran. But he did not drop the wood."

Double and Trouble scratched their heads. They scratched their backs.

"Grandfather ran all the way back to the village shouting 'Aieee!' But he did not drop the wood until he reached his mother's house."

Double Trouble stared at Anna Hibiscus with wide-wide eyes.

"Grandfather's mother heard him screaming. She saw her son jumping up and down, scratching his head and shouting 'Aieeeeee!' Grandfather's mother thought he had been stung by red ants."

Double Trouble looked at each other. That was serious.

"Then she saw tiny-tiny black ants running all over Grandfather. Those tiny-tiny ants were just as confused and frightened as Grandfather! Grandfather's mother started to laugh."

Double and Trouble clapped their hands. Double Trouble laughed!

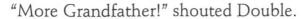

"More Grandfather!" shouted Double.

"More Grandfather!" shouted Trouble.

"More Grandfather!" said Anna's father.

Anna Hibiscus jumped. She looked
around. Everybody in
her whole entire family
was standing in the
kitchen doorway!

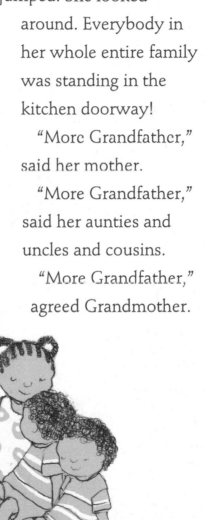

"More Grandfather,"
said her mother.

"More Grandfather,"
said her aunties and
uncles and cousins.

"More Grandfather,"
agreed Grandmother.

Then Uncle Bizi Sunday turned off the burned stew. And Anna's mother and father and uncles and aunties and cousins and Sunny Belafonte and Grandmother all sat on the floor with Anna Hibiscus and Double Trouble.

Double climbed onto his mother's lap. Trouble climbed onto his father's lap.

"Come on, amazing Anna Hibiscus," everybody said again. "More Grandfather!"

But Anna Hibiscus was shy. So Uncle Tunde spoke. "Once upon a time," said Uncle Tunde, "Grandfather was standing at a bus stop when all of a sudden a poor woman shouted 'Thief!' Somebody had stolen her purse.

Many people chased the thief, and many people comforted the woman. But our Grandfather, what did he do? When the thief could not be caught, Grandfather gave the woman the money in his own wallet."

Grandmother nodded proudly. She remembered that day well. Grandfather had to work a lot of overtime to earn back that money. They had needed it too.

The aunties wiped their eyes. They were so proud. The uncles looked at each other. They must always follow their father's example.

Double Trouble and Sunny Belafonte and all the cousins clapped. How wonderful Grandfather had been!

Everybody had a story to tell about Grandfather. Even Sunny Belafonte!

"My grandfather told me that once your grandfather was swimming in the river when he mistook a log for a crocodile..."

Everybody laughed so much at that story that they had to wipe their eyes.

The whole family shared stories about Grandfather. Double and Trouble smiled and smiled and smiled. They had been worried, but now they knew – nobody had forgotten about Grandfather. Nobody would ever forget Grandfather. They couldn't see Grandfather, but they could talk about him as much as they liked.

When Double and Trouble fell asleep, Anna's mother and father carried them to bed. The uncles and aunties and big cousins carried the little cousins to bed. Grandmother went to lie on her mat.

Anna Hibiscus looked at Sunny Belafonte. She had a smile on her face, and tears on her face too.

How was it possible to laugh and smile when Grandfather was dead?

Then Anna Hibiscus realized: "If I can smile now, then no matter what happens in my life, I will still be able to be happy."

"And that is the best thing that I could ever teach you, my daughter," said Grandfather's voice.

Anna Hibiscus told Sunny Belafonte about her happy sadness. Sunny Belafonte squeezed her hand. "That is how I feel too. My mother and grandfather are dead and my father is gone. But sometimes I am happy. Sometimes life is good."

Anna Hibiscus nodded. And her tears dropped off the corners of her smile.

Auntie Joly came downstairs to chase
Anna and Sunny up to bed. Grandmother
stopped her.

"Shh!" she said. "Amazing Anna Hibiscus
is busy growing up."

Atinuke was born in Nigeria and spent her childhood in both Africa and the UK. She works as a traditional oral storyteller in schools and theaters all over the world. Atinuke lives on a mountain overlooking the sea in West Wales. She supports the charity SOS Children's Villages.

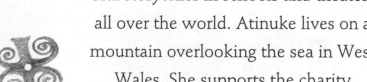

Lauren Tobia lives in Southville, Bristol. She shares her tiny house with her husband and their two yappy Jack Russell terriers. When Lauren is not drawing, she can be found drinking tea on her allotment.